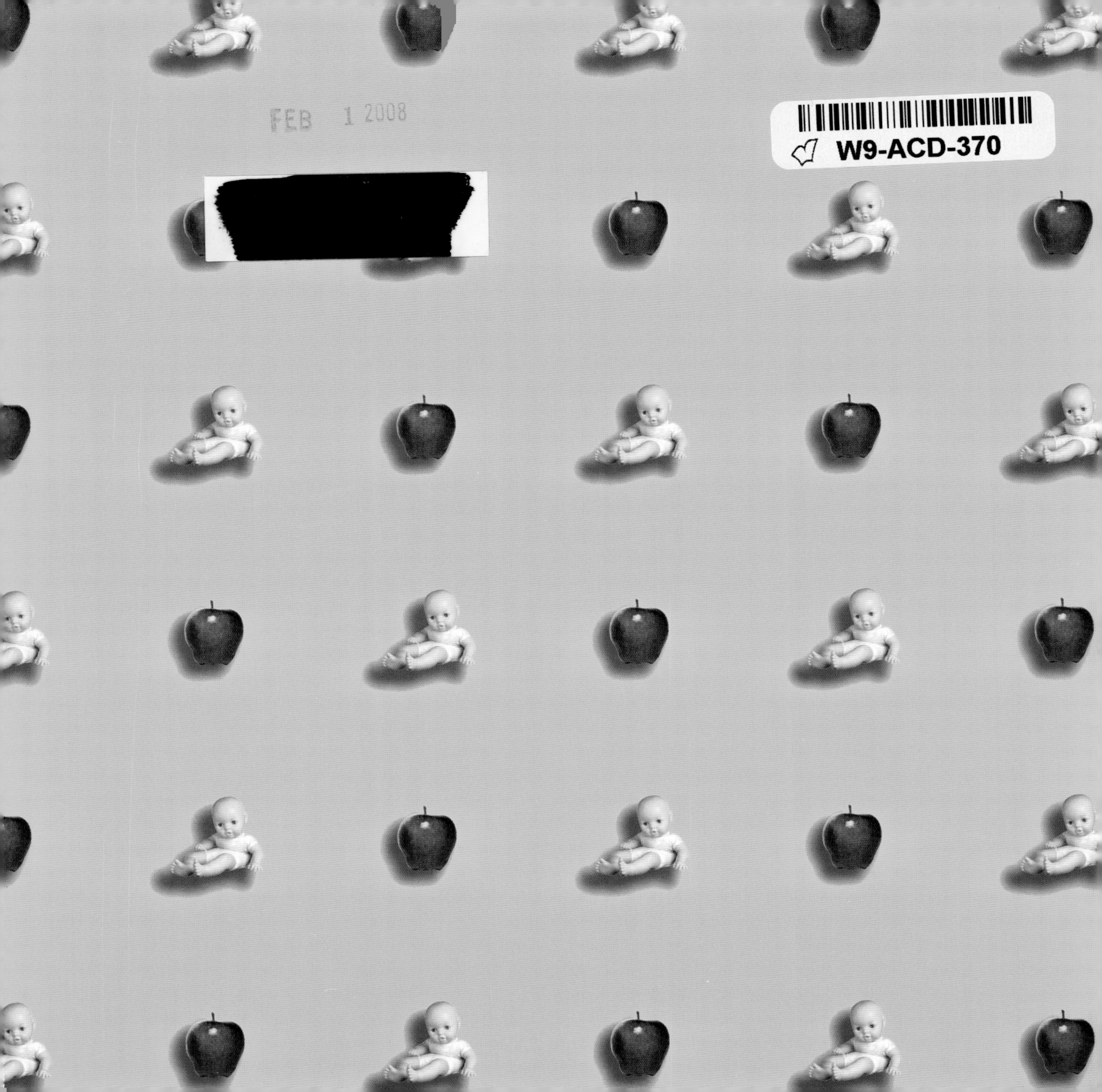

Look What I See! Where Can I Be?

In the Neighborhood

by Dia L. Michels

Photographs by
Michael J.N. Bowles

Platypus Media, LLC
Washington, DC USA
2001

For Dad,
whose vision and courage
inspire me

Look for these *Look What I See Books* by Dia L. Michels

Look What I See! Where Can I Be? At Home
Look What I See! Where Can I Be? At the Synagogue
Look What I See! Where Can I Be? On the Go in China
Look What I See! Where Can I Be? In the Neighborhood
Look What I See! Where Can I Be? With My Animal Friends

Teacher's guide available at PlatypusMedia.com

Library of Congress Cataloging-in-Publication Data

Michels, Dia L.
In the neighborhood / by Dia L. Michels; photographs by Michael J.N. Bowles.
p. cm.–(Look what I see! Where can I be?)
Summary: By viewing a detail from a photograph that is revealed on the following page, the reader is invited to guess which place Baby is visiting in the neighborhood.
ISBN 1-930775-00-8
[1. Neighborhood—Fiction. 2. City and town life—Fiction. 3. Babies—Fiction.] I. Bowles, Michael J.N., ill. II. Title.
PZ7.M5817 In 2001
[E]—dc21

00-066952

Platypus Media is committed to the promotion and protection of breastfeeding.
We donate six percent of our profits to breastfeeding organizations.

Platypus Media LLC
627 A Street NE
Washington DC 20002 USA
PlatypusMedia.com
ISBN1-930775-00-8

1 2 3 4 5 6 7 8 9

Edited by Ellen E.M. Roberts, Where Books Begin, New York, NY
Designed by Douglas Wink, Inkway Graphics, Jersey City, NJ
Produced by Millicent Fairhurst, MF Book Production Services, New York, NY

La Leche League, International, logo, used by permission
Baby Bundler, used by permission

Manufactured in the United States of America

I go everywhere
with my family
in the neighborhood.

On Monday,
I fell asleep in the wagon.

When I woke up,
I saw black seeds.

Where was I?

At the market.

On Tuesday,
I fell asleep
in the baby bundler.

When I woke up
I saw an eagle.

Where was I?

At the
post office.

Post Office
EXPRESS
MAIL

On Wednesday,
I fell asleep in my sling.

When I woke up,
I saw a fish.

Where was I?

At the
aquarium.

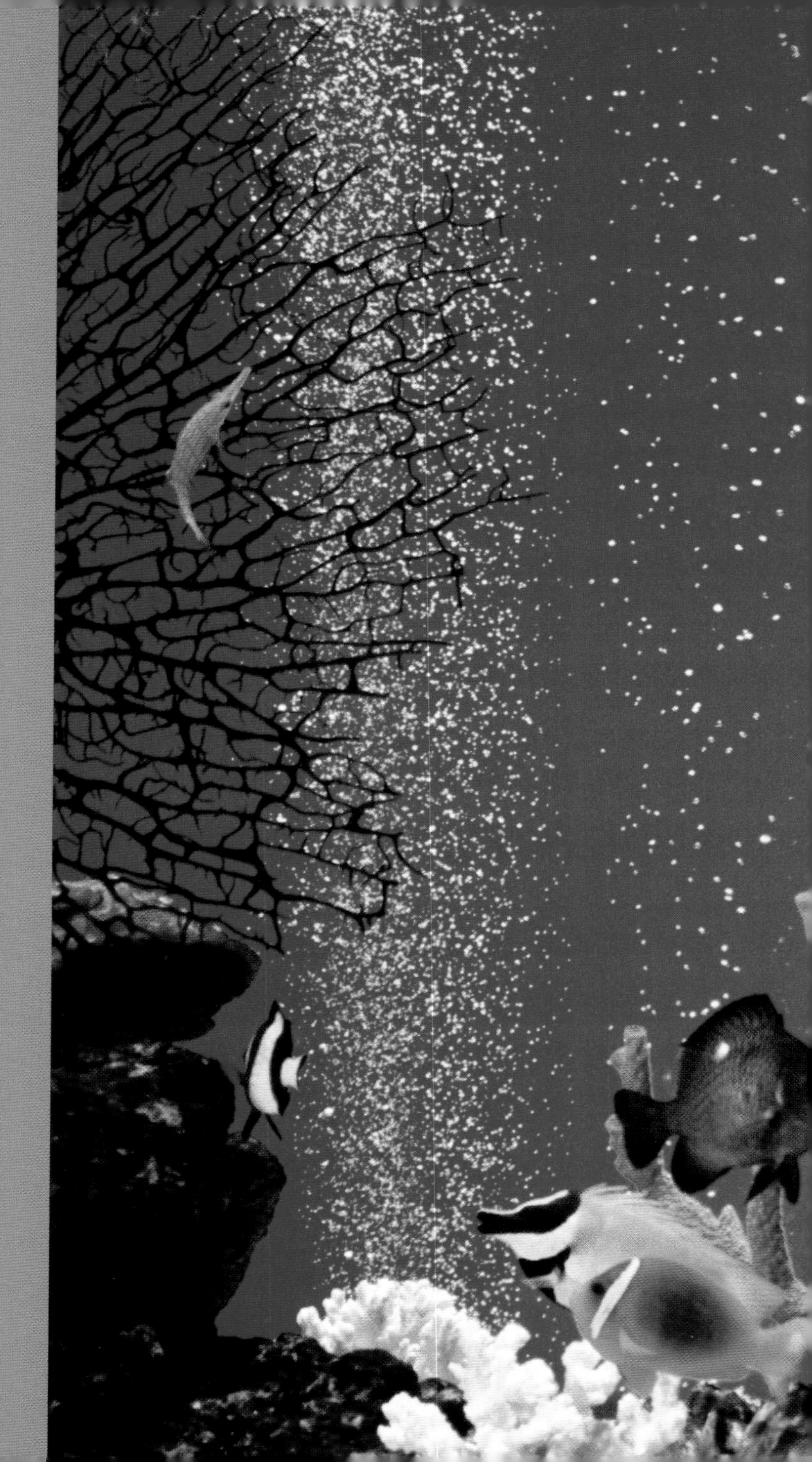

On Thursday,
I fell asleep in my stroller.

When I woke up,
I saw a tiny light.

Where was I?

At the
doctor's office.

On Friday,
I fell asleep in
my backpack.

When I woke up,
I saw flowers.

Where was I?

At the park.

On Saturday,
I fell asleep in my
front carrier.

When I woke up,
I saw a gingerbread boy.

Where was I?

At the library.

On Sunday,
I fell asleep on
my Mommy's lap.

When I woke up
I saw a shiny circle.

Where was I?

Safe and warm
in Mommy's
arms.

I am back home again
with my family
in the neighborhood.